W9-AEV-029

BiRD

BUTTERFLY

SQUIRRL

MOUSE

MiSTER BUN

AiR PLANe

SPACESHiP

CAR

BALLOON

To working parents everywhere
who bridge the distance with love
—S. B.-Q.

For my own little Boos
—B. A.

ATHENEUM BOOKS FOR YOUNG READERS
An imprint of Simon & Schuster Children's Publishing Division
1230 Avenue of the Americas, New York, New York 10020
Text copyright © 2017 by Sudipta Bardhan-Quallen
Illustrations copyright © 2017 by Bonnie Adamson
All rights reserved, including the right of reproduction in whole or in part in any form.
ATHENEUM BOOKS FOR YOUNG READERS is a registered trademark of Simon & Schuster, Inc.
Atheneum logo is a trademark of Simon & Schuster, Inc.
For information about special discounts for bulk purchases, please contact Simon & Schuster
Special Sales at 1-866-506-1949 or business@simonandschuster.com.
The Simon & Schuster Speakers Bureau can bring authors to your live event. For more
information or to book an event, contact the Simon & Schuster Speakers Bureau at
1-866-248-3049 or visit our website at www.simonspeakers.com.
Book design by Ann Bobco
The text for this book was set in Chaloops.
The illustrations for this book were rendered in watercolor and pencil.
Manufactured in China
1216 SCP
First Edition
10 9 8 7 6 5 4 3 2 1
Library of Congress Cataloging-in-Publication Data
Names: Bardhan-Quallen, Sudipta. | Adamson, Bonnie, illustrator.
Title: Rutabaga boo! / Sudipta Bardhan-Quallen ; illustrated by Bonnie Adamson.
Description: First edition. | New York : Atheneum Books for Young Readers, [2017] |
Summary: "This very young call-and-response book that calls to mind the game 'Marco Polo'
celebrates the steadfast connection between a mother and her son—even when Mom has to
be away"—Provided by publisher.
Identifiers: LCCN 2014017414 | ISBN 9781481424615 (hardcover) | ISBN 9781481424622 (eBook)
Subjects: | CYAC: Mother and child—Fiction. | Separation (Psychology)—Fiction.
Classification: LCC PZ7.B25007 Ru 2017 | DDC [E]—dc23
LC record available at http://lccn.loc.gov/2014017414

story by
Sudipta Bardhan-Quallen

Rutabaga
Boo!

pictures by Bonnie Adamson

atheneum

ATHENEUM BOOKS FOR YOUNG READERS
New York · London · Toronto · Sydney · New Delhi

Rutabaga?

Boo!

Rutabaga!

Boo!

Rutabaga?

Boo.

Ruta...

Boo!

Rutabaga?

I always love you.

BIRD

BUTTERFLY

SQUIRReL

MOUSE

MISTeR BUN

AIRPLANe

SPACESHIP

CAR

BALLOON